John Witt
Illustrated by Bryan Cooke

Hatless

Pretty Road Press
Folsom, California

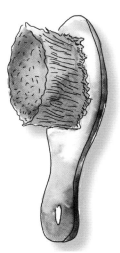

Pretty Road Press
P.O. Box 273
Folsom, California 95763-0273
www.PrettyRoadPress.com

This book was manufactured with materials that are in compliance with the Consumer Product Safety Improvement Act, ensuring the book is safe for children to enjoy.

Published 2010
Printed in the United States of America
13 12 11 10   5 4 3 2 1

ISBN 978-0-9826014-0-2

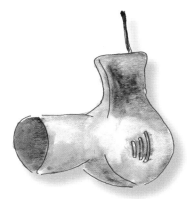

This book was typeset in 18 point Arial.
Illustrations were created with watercolor and ink on watercolor paper.

Marco's hair was always out of control.
After years of trying to tame it, he simply gave up.

He told his mom,
"I think I might need a hat."

"Why do you need
a hat, Marco?" she asked.

"My hair is just too crazy!"

The next morning Marco and his mother
walked to the local thrift store, hunting for a hat.

Marco spotted the ideal cap — a warm,
colorful, odd-looking thing.

Marco's mother kindly paid with two quarters,
and Marco moved the hat to his head.

He tucked in his crazy hair.
Instantly he fell in love with his hat.

He called the hat his friend, and
he wore it everywhere he went.

He wore it to school.

He wore it in bed.

He wore it at the pool.

He even wore it at church,

where he sang loudly and got strange looks.

Winter, spring, summer, and fall — whenever you saw Marco, you also saw his hat and a few strands of his crazy hair.

People yelled and pointed.
They made fun of Marco.

"Look at the kid with the
weird hat!" some would shout.

Marco didn't care. He loved his hat. Insults wouldn't stop him from wearing it proudly on top of his head.

One day when Marco went to the amusement park with his family, everything took a turn for the worst.

He was riding the roller coaster when the wind stole Marco's hat right off of his head.

Marco's stomach dropped, not from the fall of the roller coaster, but from the loss of his beloved hat.

When the ride was over, Marco and his family scoured the park for hours, clinging to the hope his hat would appear.

He had no success.

For the first time in more than a year,
Marco would go home hatless.

During the drive home, he realized he would never see his hat again. Tears streamed down his cheeks.

Marco went straight to bed that night.

He got out of bed the next morning seeing his dad holding a brand new hat.

"Look what I have for you, Marco," his dad said.

But Marco selfishly refused the gift.
He wanted nothing else but his trusty old hat.

Marco didn't know that his long lost friend was actually beginning an adventure of its own.

The wind swept Marco's hat high into the clouds.

Gravity pulled it down into a river.

The hat leapt off a water fall and

swam into the ocean . . .

...was devoured by the waves,

then plopped onto the beach...

...and finally scooped up by an oblivious bird,

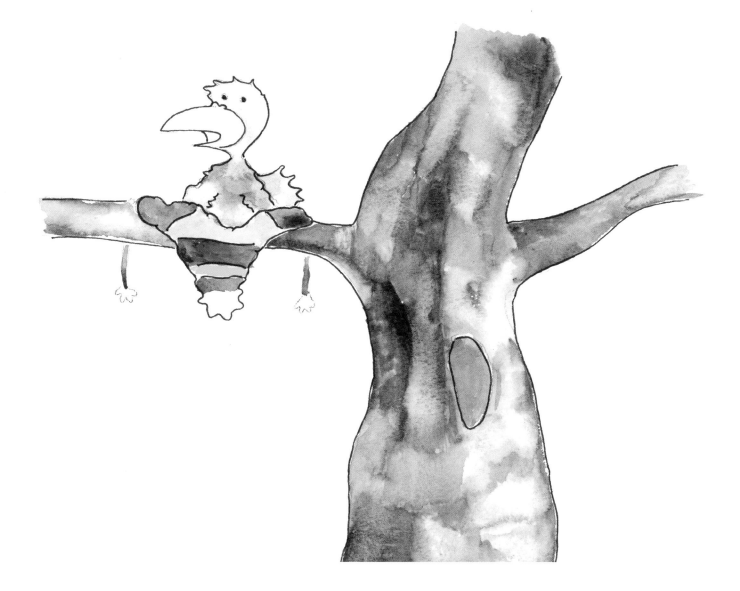

who turned it into a nest in a tree.

Weeks later Marco and his mother walked
to the Public Market on the coldest day of winter.

Marco was hatless.
His crazy hair kept some of the cold away.

He was still a little teary over the loss of his hat
until he and his mother crossed the street.

Marco stopped. His heart pounded quickly.

Sitting on the ground, under a tall tree,
was a friend he knew well.

It was worn and torn, tattered and battered,
weathered and feathered, once lost and now found.

There was Marco's long lost hat — the very one that had
kept him warm, kept him safe, and kept his hair contained.

He jumped for joy and screamed as he placed his friend back on his head. "I found it! I found it!" he shouted as he continued on toward the market.

He smiled and skipped. But his smile drooped as he neared the stores.

He spotted an elderly bald man,

shivering and sitting against a building.

Marco noticed his own reflection
in the Public Market window behind the man.

He saw his rain boots, pants,
a warm coat — and his favorite hat.

Without another thought, Marco walked closer to the shivering man and asked, "Are you cold, mister?"

The bald man nodded softly.

Marco lifted his hat off his crazy hair and placed it right on top of the man's shiny bald head.

The man smiled and played Marco a song.
Marco smiled back while his hair sprang back into action.

Never had Marco felt so good about being hatless.